DINOSAUR
Funbook

Written and Illustrated by
WILLIAM R. JOHNSON

Cenozoic Era
The age of man and mammals
65 million years

Mesozoic Era
THE AGE OF DINOSAURS
167 million years

Paleozoic Era
The age of primitive reptiles,
amphibians, fishes & invertebrates
350 million years

 TROUBADOR PRESS

a subsidiary of

PRICE STERN SLOAN
Los Angeles

CONTENTS

20 19 18 17 16 15 14 13 12

ISBN: 0-8431-1704-

INTRODUCTION TO THE DINOSAURS

Dinosaurs lived 65 to 225 million years ago. In the past hundred or so years scientists have found many dinosaur bones and teeth and have put them together to make whole skeletons. You may have seen them in museums. The word dinosaur comes from two old Latin words: *dino* meaning "terrible" and *saur* meaning "lizard"; therefore, *dinosaur* means "terrible lizard."

We know, in fact, that dinosaurs were not lizards and most of them were not fierce or terrible at all. They were not even all giant beasts; some were no larger than today's common fowl.

There are different categories of dinosaurs. They can be divided into meat eating and plant eating, and according to body differences. Some dinosaurs had hip bones like a reptile, others had hip bones like a bird. The dinosaurs with reptile hips are also divided into two kinds: theropods (ther-uh-pods) and sauropods (sor-uh-pods).

The theropods walked on two legs and were meat eaters. They ranged in size from two to 15 meters (approximately six to 50 feet). The sauropods were usually giant beasts that ate plants and walked on all fours.

Then there were the two kinds of dinosaurs with bird-like hips, the ornithopods (or-NITH-uh-pods) and the armed dinosaurs. Both of these were plant eating animals. The ornithopods walked on their hind legs and the armed dinosaurs walked on all four legs.

Dinosaurs were not all here on earth at the same time. Even the dinosaurs in this book were not all contemporaries of each other. Dinosaur life evolved during what is known as the Mesozoic Era, when many varied types of amphibians developed.

Within the Mesozoic Era, we locate three periods of their evolution: The Triassic period came first (190 million to 225 million years ago); at this time earliest reptiles came out of the seas and seemingly spread to all continents. Then came the Jurassic period (136 to 190 million years ago), when the first giant dinosaurs began to roam the earth. The big carnivorous—meat eating—types presumably preyed on the even larger herbivorous, or plant eating, dinosaurs. The marine dinosaurs, like ichthyosaurs and plesiosaurs, still swam the shallow seas of both hemispheres and the flying reptiles (pterosaurs) made their appearance. The bird-like and the duck-billed dinosaurs ranged all over the world during the Jurassic period.

Dinosaur evolution climaxed during the Cretaceous period (65 to 136 million years ago). The herbivorous ornithischian dinosaurs were by then seen regularly on all continents and sea lanes. Unluckily, they were seen as easy pickings by hungry, fierce tyrannosaurs, last of the giant carnivores. Even so, the duck-billed creatures outnumbered any other species of dinosaur.

It was the dinosaurs' world for 167 million years. Man and mammal have not yet been around that long.

TYRANNOSAURUS REX

(ty-ran-o-SAWR-us)

Tyrannosaurus was one of the largest and most fearful of all dinosaurs. Almost 15 meters (47 feet) in length from head to tail, it stood over six and one-half meters (20 feet) tall when erect on its hind legs.

Tyrannosaurus was a theropod, with reptile hips. The name *Tyrannosaurus rex* means "tyrant lizard king." It was one of the few dinosaurs that was actually flesh-eating. It lived at the close of the Cretaceous period, just before the dinosaurs died out.

Built for the hunt, *Tyrannosaurus* possessed powerful legs to pursue, front claws to hold and head and jaws to eat the prey. *Tyrannosaurus* had an enormous head with saw-bladed, dagger-like teeth, 15 centimeters (six inches) long. Even its powerful tail was probably used as a weapon.

Despite *Tyrannosaurus'* mighty legs, its stride was only one meter, but it could easily catch victims such as *Triceratops* and other slow-moving beasts. *Tyrannosaurus* has a rather unusual leg structure: besides the usual knee joint an equally important joint existed between shin and foot.

The foot had four toes, three pointing forward and one placed higher and pointing backward, just below the second knee joint. The middle toes of the foot were the longest.

Two finger claws extended from Rex's spindly arms, similar in length to a human's.

He was king wherever he roamed in the Cretaceous period.

FIND THE TRUE TYRANNOSAURUS REX

Here are six different tyrannosaurs but only one is a *true Tyranno-saurus rex.* To help you find it there is an error of some kind in each drawing but one. Find the true *Rex.*

Answers on page 46

REX 1

REX 2

REX 3

REX 4

REX 5

REX 6

HE EATS LIKE A KING!

On his way home from work this *Tyrannosaurus rex* often stops off for a bite to eat, or six. But he must never go to the same place twice. Can you show old *Rex* the way to go—not missing any but going to each only once. And then home. It is a fact—*Tyrannosaurus rex* eats like a king.

Answer on page 46

home

THIRTEEN T WORDS!

Thirteen words beginning with the letter "t" are hidden among all those other letters. Can you find them? Some of the words read across and some read down.

Answers on page 46

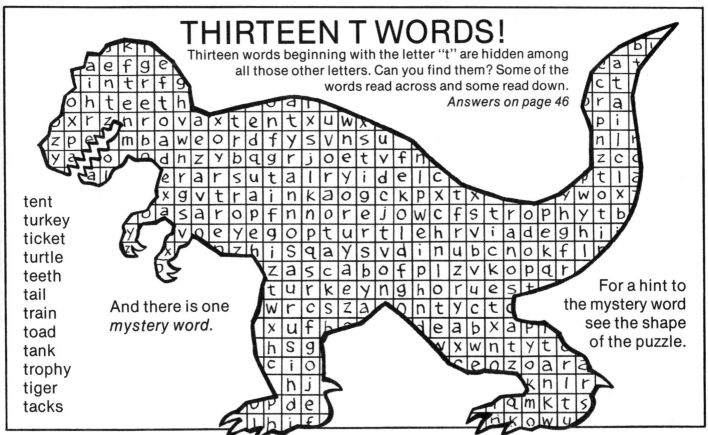

tent
turkey
ticket
turtle
teeth
tail
train
toad
tank
trophy
tiger
tacks

And there is one *mystery word.*

For a hint to the mystery word see the shape of the puzzle.

7

BRONTOSAURUS

(bront-o-SAWR-us)

One of the largest, *Brontosaurus* is also one of the best known of all dinosaurs. It lived about 130 million years ago during the Jurassic period of the Mesozoic Age.

Brontosaurus reached a length of 20 to 20 meters (70 to 80 feet) and weighed about 27 metric tons (30 tons). This dinosaur always walked on all four feet. Its footprint covered more than one-third of a square meter (one square foot) of ground and the earth shook when it walked. For this reason it was named *Brontosaurus*, meaning "thunder lizard." *Brontosaurus* is also known, more correctly, by the name *Apatosaurus*.

With its huge body and small head, the brontosaur was until recently considered slow moving, cold-blooded and slow witted. Many scientists now challenge that belief. They say that dinosaurs, including brontosaurs, were in fact agile, warm-blooded and smarter than supposed.

If dinosaurs were warm-blooded that would help explain why they so dominated their time. The difference between cold-blooded reptiles (turtles, snakes) and warm-blooded mammals (humans, dogs) is that mammals can regulate their own body temperature. Reptiles must take on the temperature of the surrounding environment, the way a lizard soaks up energy from the sun. When warm-blooded and cold-blooded creatures compete for habitat, the warm-blooded wins out. Their bodies require more food so they are more aggressive. And they are relentless hunters. With their built-in furnaces, they can move more freely in an area.

DINOSAUR RIDDLES

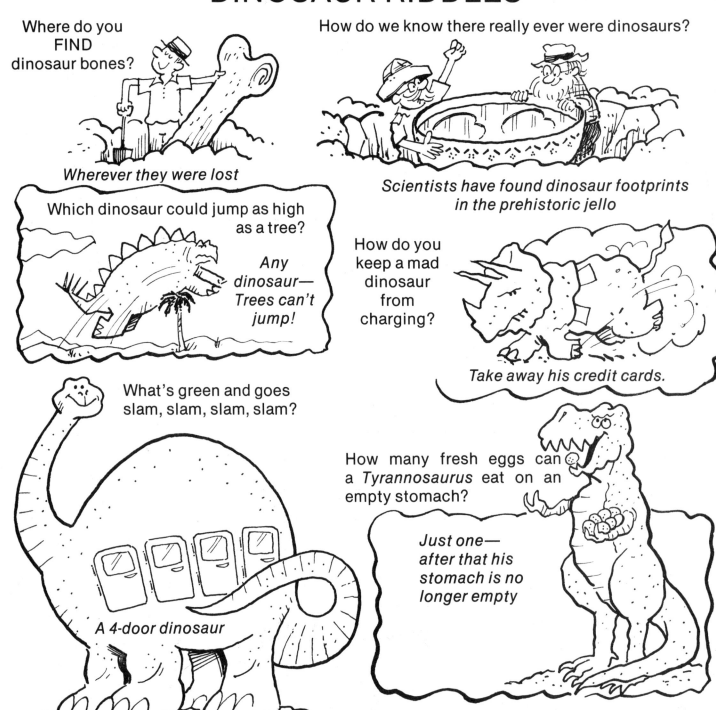

Where do you FIND dinosaur bones?

Wherever they were lost

How do we know there really ever were dinosaurs?

Scientists have found dinosaur footprints in the prehistoric jello

Which dinosaur could jump as high as a tree?

Any dinosaur— Trees can't jump!

How do you keep a mad dinosaur from charging?

Take away his credit cards.

What's green and goes slam, slam, slam, slam?

A 4-door dinosaur

How many fresh eggs can a *Tyrannosaurus* eat on an empty stomach?

Just one— after that his stomach is no longer empty

THUNDER LIZARD CROSSWORD

Down

1. Related to the _____ .
2. Official name of the species.
5. Makes _____ when he walks.
6. Lizards are _____ .
7. Dinosaurs have a _____ brain.

Across

3. *Brontosaurus* weighed about 20 _____ .
4. Real name of the "thunder lizard."
8. Favorite food.
9. It had a _____ neck and tail.
10. Spent much of its life in the _____ .

Answers on page 46

11

STEGOSAURUS

(steg-o-SAWR-us)

Stegosaurus was a typical armored reptile dinosaur. These plated reptiles, or stegosaurs, were about six to seven and one-half meters (20 to 25 feet) from nose to end of tail and almost three meters (eight feet) high at the hips. They had high arched bodies and carried their heads low. In all stegosaurs the forelegs were about one-half the size of the hind legs.

Stegosaurus means "roofed lizard." A plant eater, it lived along with the *Brontosaurus* during the Jurassic period.

Stegosaurus is one of the most curious of the dinosaurs because of its armor: upright body plates stood in two rows along the middle of its back and four sharp spikes rose from the end of its tail. These were *Stegosaurus'* only means of defense. The plates could probably defend against attack and the spikes could do damage as the tail lashed about.

Stegosaurus is noted for the very small size of its brain, about 70 grams (two and one-half ounces) compared with its total bulk weight of two to four metric tons. But some scientists think that a "second brain" was located on its back, near the spinal cord, which controlled the bony plates, causing them to clap together in warning, anger or even attracting the opposite sex. Other scientists insist this nerve (sacral plexus) is *not* a second brain. So questions still remain as science continues to learn more about dinosaurs.

THE STEGOSAURUS SCRAMBLE—
WORD GAMES

Take the scrambled letters and use whichever is necessary to complete the words shown below in Game 1.

There are 3 word games here:
1. Missing letters
   2. Scrambled words with a missing letter
      3. How many words can you make?
      Answers on page 46

Game 1. Complete these words using any letters from *Stegosaurus* above.

__ cho __ l
__ uest
__ __ gle
__ oat
__ s __ rich
__ ppl __
__ kelel __
__ af __
__ mbr __ ll __
__ w __ rd

Game 2. Make words out of these scrambled letters and one missing letter from *Stegosaurus* above.

ali__or
eahce__r
ba__rd
rtesa__et
mai__blx
ti__tra
irc__rfat
cr__thc
tgi__e
m__cis
h__ore

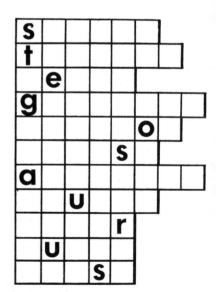

Game 3. How many words (three letters or more) can you make from *Stegosaurus?* There are at least 29. Finding 20 words is good!

Answers on page 46

_____   _____   _____   _____
_____   _____   _____   _____
_____   _____   _____   _____
_____   _____   _____   _____
_____   _____   _____   _____

READ THE REBUS— A DINOSAUR STORY
Add and subtract the letters and words illustrated, as directed by the *plus* and *minus* signs to read the story. The boxes tell you how many letters are in each word.

Answer on page 46

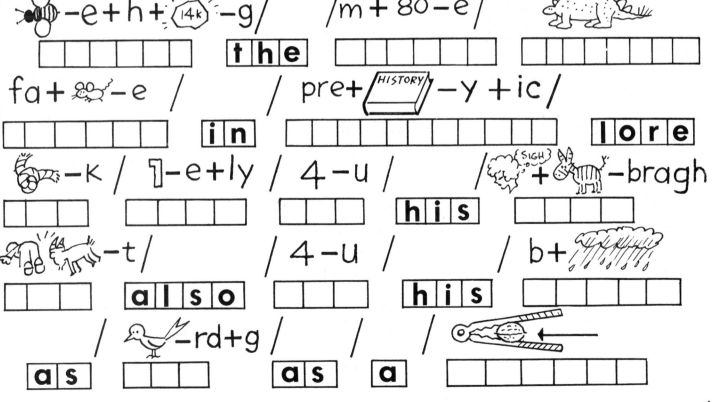

CORYTHOSAURUS

(kor-ith-o-SAWR-us)

Corythosaurus, meaning "helmeted lizard," was so named because the top of its skull looked like a Corinthian (Ancient Greek) helmet. It belonged to a great family of duck-billed dinosaurs (*Trachodontidae*). All the duck-billed dinosaurs lived during the Cretaceous period, the last of the three periods of the Mesozoic Age. All had the same general body type and habits, living in or near water and eating plants. They differed primarily in the structure of their skulls, and *Corythosaurus* was unique.

Scientists still wonder about the purpose of the elegantly formed skull helmet. At first, it was believed that *Corythosaurus* could breathe under water through channels in the helmet, but this is now doubted. More likely it was a form of hearing aid which helped the creature learn of oncoming enemies. *Corythosaurus* also had a keen sense of smell, very good eyesight and a loud voice.

Although this duck-billed dinosaur averaged up to 10½ meters (35 feet) in length and stood five meters (17 feet) tall when erect on its hind legs, it was no match for the flesh eaters of its time.

Trachodon was the most abundant of all dinosaurs—at least as numerous as deer are today. Their remains are most commonly found in former lake and marshy areas of North America.

Among their remains are found a rich supply of teeth. In some species, twenty-five hundred teeth have been found in the skull and jaws! These were usually arranged so that when one wore out another below replaced it.

MATCH THE PAIRS

Some of these lovely beasts have a look-alike in the group. Can you pick out each identical pair?

Answers on page 46

1.

2.

3.

5.

6.

7.

9.

10

11.

13.

14.

15.

WHICH TYRANNOSAURUS GETS THE MEAL?

Trace the maze to see who gets there first—only one can win—Will it be Blacky, Whitey, Spotty or Stripe?

Answer on page 47

STRUTHIOMIMUS

(strooth-ee-o-MIME-us)

Struthiomimus means "ostrich mimic" and it is one of a wide species of dinosaurs known as the "ostrich dinosaurs." Because animals that look alike usually function similarly, the ostrich dinosaurs probably acted much like the ostrich of today.

Struthiomimus was obviously a rapid runner. Its body development was especially unique for this: a flap of skin connecting the arms to the body may have acted as an airfoil when the beast ran.

About four meters (14 feet) from head to tail and almost three meters (nine and one-half feet) tall, it had a small hard beack, delicate toothless head, large eyes and a long slender tail and neck.

Struthiomimus ate fruits, other vegetation and perhaps the eggs of other dinosaurs in the Cretaceous period some 63 to 135 million years ago in North America.

The creature is a key figure in the cold-blooded against warm-blooded dinosaur theories. While its bone structure indicates it could dash to speeds of almost 80 kph (50 mph), those who believe it to have been reptilian put its maximum speed at about three kph (one mph). This difference feeds the current debate over whether dinosaurs were cold-blooded (ectothermic), as scientists have believed for over 100 years, or warm-blooded (endothermic), as is becoming more popular today.

Color in numbers 1-10 to disclose the mystery picture.

ANTONYM ANAGRAMS

UP... DOWN...

You can change the top three words to their opposite or *antonym* in four steps. Change only one letter at each step. Each step must make a word too.

Answers on page 47

An antonym is a word that means the opposite of another word.

COLD **CAME** **WALK**

_____ _____ _____

_____ _____ _____

_____ _____ _____

WARM **WENT** **RIDE**

22

STARRING ☆ STRUTHIOMIMUS

This dinosaur is famous for acting like an ostrich. Now you can help with its latest act—QUICK CHANGE WORDS!

Rules: 1. Do the crosswords across and down.

2. Then add one letter in each shaded box to form new words *across* and *down*.

HINT! ADD SAME LETTER ALL AROUND.

ACROSS
1. Opposite of high
2. Meat; not kid's favorite
3. Run with a long stride
4. A swelling or bump
5. To bind securely with rope

Answers on page 47

DOWN
1. To be without
2. Part of the mouth
3. A noose
4. Thick, luxurious
5. Upper legs when sitting

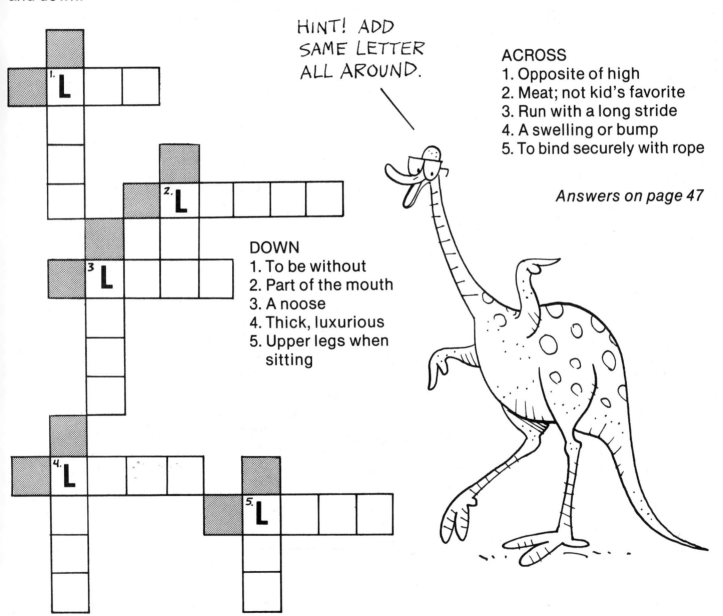

PTERANODON

(ter-AN-o-don)

Pteranodon, from the order *Pterosauria,* is known from both the Jurassic and Cretaceous periods. Both pterosaurs and birds developed from the thecodants, a species of earliest dinosaurs. The pterosaurs, however, were the least successful of the two and did not survive the Cretaceous period. Probably warm-blodded, their distinctive covering of feathers conserved heat for their bodies and blood.

Pteranodon was one of the largest winged animals of all time, with a wingspread of over seven meters (25 feet) and a long crest extending back from the head. This crest is sometimes considered a "steering vane."

Its wing was probably quite vulnerable to rupture, much more so than the wings of bats or birds. Flying dinosaurs from the Jurassic period had long tails which had shrunk to a stub by the time of *Pteranodon.*

The skeleton of the flying dinosaur was light with air-filled bones. Each gauze-like elongated wing was composed of a membrane of skin attached to and supported by the arm and one strong finger on each hand.

Called a "truly gigantic kite," it flew principally by soaring and gliding, since the wings lacked the flexibility and durability of bird wings. As most *Pteranodon* remains have been found in marine deposits, it is assumed that they lived along ocean shores, roosting on cliffs from which they would glide off into the wind.

DINOSAURS DOT-TO-DOT

Follow the dots from A to Z, then on from a to I. Start again at 1 and go to 61. When you're done you'll see the difference.

Answer on page 47

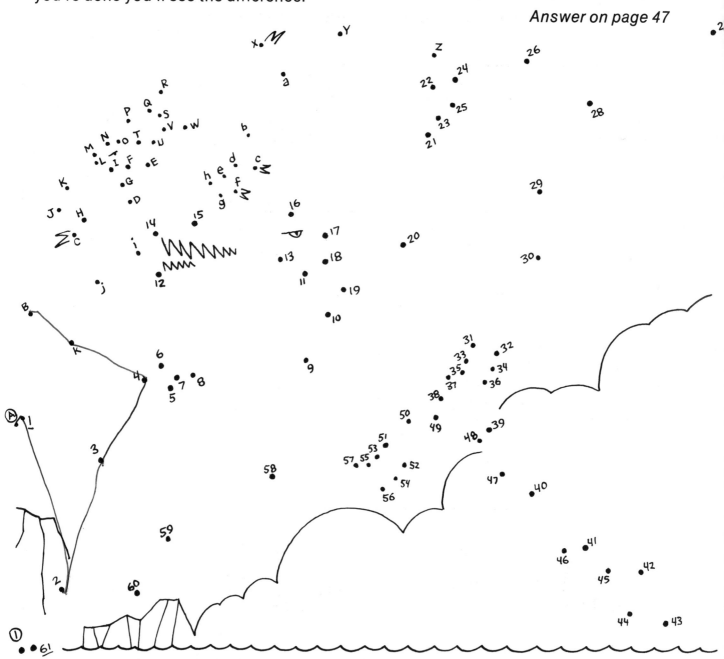

MATCH THE ANTONYMS GAME

An *antonym* is *not* another dinosaur name. An antonym is a word that is *opposite* from another word. Think of a word for each picture, write it and then write its antonym. All are illustrated. The dashes indicate how many letters are in each word.

Answers on page 47

ELASMOSAURUS

(e-LAZ-mo-sawr-us)

Plesiosaurs were swimming reptiles that lived in inland seas or coastal waters while dinosaurs roamed the land. Their limbs were paddle-like flippers and they swam like turtles, although they may have used their hind limbs for more than just steering. Both hip and shoulder sections in the plesiosaurs have small upper portions and very large lower portions. As the relation of upper body to body weight is important for moving on land, it seems unlikely that a plesiosaur's limbs could easily have supported its bulk; therefore, a plesiosaur rarely, if ever, came out of the water. Still, it may have struggled on land to lay eggs, much as turtles do.

During the Jurassic period the plesiosaur family split, evolving into two main branches. In one, the head grew larger and the neck shorter. In the other, culminating in the Cretaceous *Elasmosaurus* 70 million years ago, the neck became longer and longer and the tail shorter, until in the 13 meter (43 foot) *Elasmosaurus,* half of the reptile was neck.

Too bulky to be a rapid swimmer, *Elasmosaurus* would move toward its prey with neck curved and head held back. It could strike forward quickly, the heavy body holding fast and the head snaring the prey.

Elasmosaurus is often depicted as the model of the famous Loch Ness monster of Scotland, a plesiosaur believed to be trapped in an inland sea.

NESSIE'S MESSAGE FROM LOCH NESS

From somewhere in the bottomless depths of the famous Loch Ness of Scotland has come a message. But first you must break the mysterious code. The empty boxes at the top will give you the message when completed. To break the code fill in the blanks below by answering each question A to G. The coded letter will then be solved—as C-1 (see circled sample). You'll like the message.

Answer on page 48

HERE IS THE MESSAGE:

1	2	3	4		5	6		7	8	9	10		11	12	13	14	15	16		17	18		19	20	21	22
H																										
C	A	C	A		B	B		G	F	E	D	,	D	A	G	G	F	C		G	D		E	F	E	A

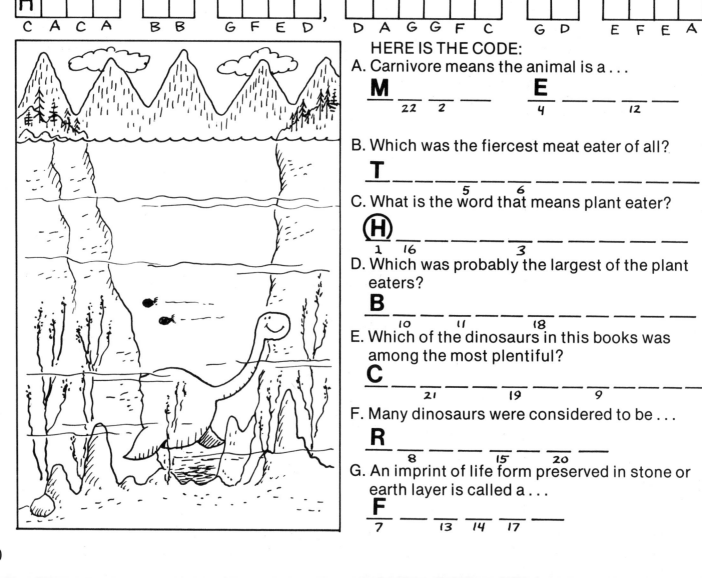

HERE IS THE CODE:

A. Carnivore means the animal is a . . .

M _ _ _   E _ _ _
22 2   4   12

B. Which was the fiercest meat eater of all?

T _ _ _ _ _ _ _ _ _ _ _
       5   6

C. What is the word that means plant eater?

(H) _ _ _ _ _ _ _ _
1 16   3

D. Which was probably the largest of the plant eaters?

B _ _ _ _ _ _ _ _ _
  10 11   18

E. Which of the dinosaurs in this books was among the most plentiful?

C _ _ _ _ _ _ _ _ _ _ _
  21   19   9

F. Many dinosaurs were considered to be . . .

R _ _ _ _ _ _ _
  8   15 20

G. An imprint of life form preserved in stone or earth layer is called a . . .

F _ _ _ _
7 13 14 17

MATCH HOW THEY MOVE

Pictured here are animals from then and now. See if you can match the movements of the prehistoric animals and the animals of today. Write the name of each animal in its proper column.

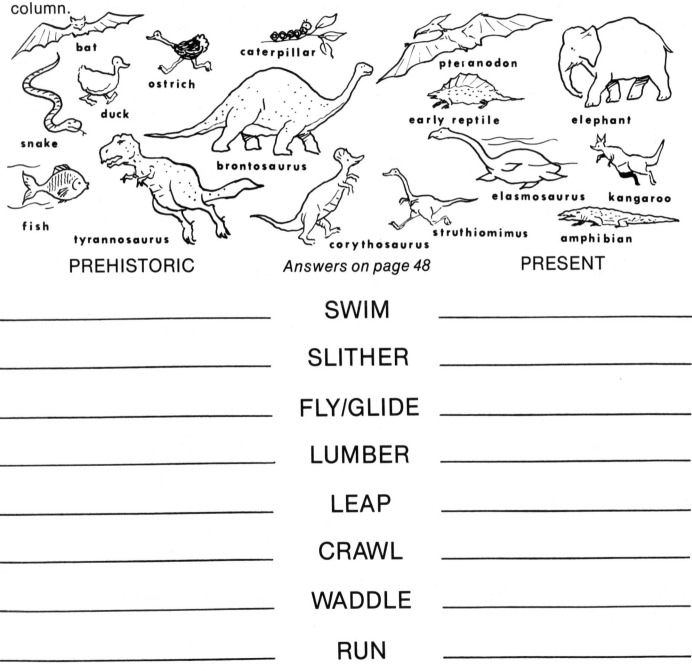

bat

ostrich

caterpillar

pteranodon

duck

early reptile

elephant

snake

brontosaurus

elasmosaurus

kangaroo

fish

tyrannosaurus

struthiomimus

amphibian

corythosaurus

PREHISTORIC

Answers on page 48

PRESENT

PREHISTORIC		PRESENT
_____	SWIM	_____
_____	SLITHER	_____
_____	FLY/GLIDE	_____
_____	LUMBER	_____
_____	LEAP	_____
_____	CRAWL	_____
_____	WADDLE	_____
_____	RUN	_____

ARCHAEOPTERYX

(ar-kea-OP-ter-ex)

The oldest known bird is *Archaeopteryx,* or "ancient wing." Unlike later birds, it had teeth and a long reptile-like yet feathered tail. Although *Archaeopteryx* had all the basics of a bird of flight it probably could barely fly if at all. Since its skeleton is closely related to that of certain Mesozoic reptiles, it undoubtedly derived from dinosaur-like ancestors.

One of the most famous fossils ever found is the near-perfect form of the *Archaeopteryx* showing a skeleton with wings, body, tail and feathers, found in the Upper Jurassic layers of limestone in Bavaria.

Archaeopteryx was about the size of today's common fowl. In the illustration here a dinosaur, known as *Ornitholestes* (or-nith-o-LES-tees), snatches one. Living in the last part of the Jurassic period, *Ornitholestes* led the way for the giant flesh-eaters of later times. It was about two meters (six feet) in length. Alert and fast-moving, it fed on smaller animals and grabbed birds like *Archaeopteryx* in "flight."

This bird is a main character in the warm-blooded (endothermic) against cold-blooded (ectothermic) debate. The question is raised in this case by paleontologist J. H. Ostrom. He says: "A cold-blooded creature with feathers would be shielded from the energy source vital to its continued existence. Therefore, feathers could not have appeared on a cold-blooded creature. The *Archaeopteryx must* have been warm-blooded. . . ."

ARCHAEOPTERYX WORD SEARCH

Find the thirteen missing words. They all begin with *ARCHAEOPTERYX*. We'll start you o
with other words *across.* You supply the synonyms reading *down.*

Answers on page 4

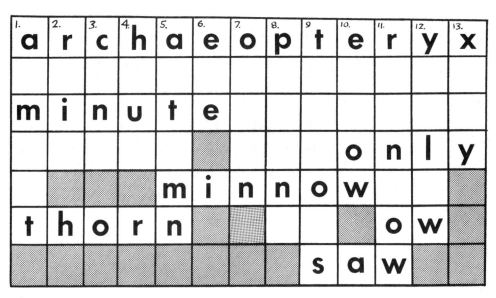

1.	2.	3.	4.	5.	6.	7.	8.	9.	10.	11.	12.	13.
a	r	c	h	a	e	o	p	t	e	r	y	x
m	i	n	u	t	e							
									o	n		y
				m	i	n	n	o	w			
t	h	o	r	n						o	w	
								s	a	w		

FIND THE WORDS
READING DOWN!

SPEAKING OF FINDING WORDS:

Here's some *old* words to find. There are nine words with "old"
in them here (example: *GOLD*). Can you find them?

a	b	c	e	j	m	e	f	t	h	i	k	u	t	x	c
g	o	l	d	f	p	q	y	o	i	d	m	s	e	a	f
c	l	b	p	g	a	m	o	l	d	r	h	a	d	l	o
s	d	j	u	k	g	e	z	d	d	l	o	s	d	a	l
p	g	s	t	e	x	y	a	c	q	g	l	d	i	e	d
a	b	e	p	w	u	v	k	i	e	l	d	l	o	c	t
m	r	s	t	b	a	f	e	w	h	a	v	u	g	y	z

Synonyms of:
1. nearly
2. shower of water
3. walking stick
4. 60 minutes
5. fall of the year
6. evening
7. frequently
8. father or mother
9. sinews attaching
   muscles
10. joint of the arm
11. arch of color
    (in the sky)
12. primary color
13. medical photo

The words may read up, down, forward and backward.

ADD UP A SURPRISE MESSAGE

First you must add or subtract to break the code, then substitute each result for a coded letter . . . the message is a surprise.

Answer on page 48

Here's the code:

1	2	3	4	5	6	7	8	9	10	11	12	13	14	15	16	17	18	19	20	21	22	23	24	25	26
a	b	c	d	e	f	g	h	i	j	k	l	m	n	o	p	q	r	s	t	u	v	w	x	y	z

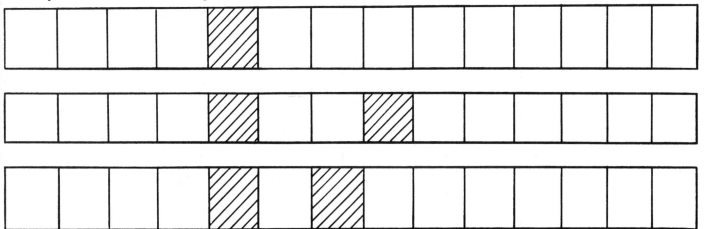

Write your decoded message here:

PROTOCERATOPS

(pro-toe-SER-at-ops)

The name means "forerunner of the horned face." *Protoceratops,* from the early Cretaceous period, is probably the direct ancestor of the huge *Triceratops* and the other horned faces: *Monoclonius, Chasmosaurus* and *Styracosaurus.* Yet the only *Protoceratops* fossils found have been about two meters (six feet) in length and about one meter (three feet) in height.

This small, plant-eating dinosaur became famous to world science when some of its eggs were found among its fossils in the deserts of Mongolia some years ago. This was the very first proof of the long-standing theory that at least some dinosaurs hatched from eggs like turtles.

While the public flocked eagerly to the eggs and fossils exhibit at the 1933 Chicago World's Fair and at the Texas Centennial Exposition, many left the display in disappointment. After always believing that dinosaurs were huge and terrible beasts, people felt let down by the dinosaurs' size. The eggs were only about 15 centimeters (six inches) long, resembling chunky Idaho potatoes. Who could accept such a little dinosaur?

Science has accepted the little fellow, regarding it as one of the most remarkable dinosaur finds. A full series of fossil bones has since been found, showing *Protoceratops'* skull development from a newly hatched baby to an adult. These bones, revealing that the frill at the back of the skull was absent in the new-born, represent developmental changes not found in fossil bones of any other dinosaur to date.

SEQUENCE THESE PHOTO PICTURES

"Sequence" means to put in the proper order. Use logic and good sense. Number each group 1 to 4 in sequence.

Answers on page 48

PETE PROTOCERATOPS NAMES HIS SON

What did he name the little tyke? To find out, fill in the antonyms (opposites) to the words reading across. You'll find the answer reading number 1 *down.* Or . . .

Answers on page 48

ACROSS

1. poor
2. close
3. down
4. late
5. sad
6. dumb

MEANWHILE, MRS. PROTOCERATOPS HIDES HER EGGS

By now you know that some dinosaurs were egg layers and some were egg stealers. Help Mrs. P. go all the way around without repeating a visit or missing any.

Answer on page 48

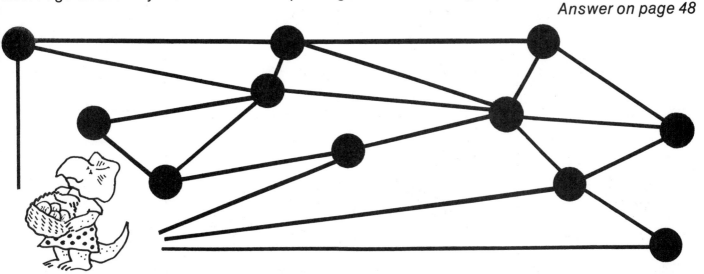

ANKYLOSAURUS

(an-kyle-o-SAWR-us)

The name *Ankylosaurus* means "curved lizard" or "stiff lizard." Stiff or curved, *Ankylosaurus* was a walking fortress, completely covered with bony armor to protect itself from the bigger, stronger flesh-eating dinosaurs.

A plant eater, it was about six meters (20 feet) in length, two meters (six feet) wide and almost two meters (five feet) high. The skull was large with an extra layer of bony plates. The whole body was also fringed with sharp spikes and the tail was a club-like weapon.

This armored tank of the Cretaceous period actually had little to worry about when he was confronted by fierce *Tyrannosaurus*. One good hit from that huge club of a tail would likely stifle the interest of the hungriest of fierce meat-eaters.

Ankylosaurus lived mostly in the Upper Cretaceous period. Although looking awkward and clumsy, the ankylosaurs got around very well. Fossils have been found in England, China, South Africa, United States and Canada. Yet ankylosaurs were similar to giant tortoises in movement and habit.

As is the case of all dinosaurs, there are variations and varieties. In two English ankylosaurs (*Acanthopholis* and *Polacanthus*), the heads and limbs were not armored but spikes and upstanding bony plates extended along the center of the back and tail. North America produced several more advanced and fully protected forms: *Nodosaurus, Edmontonia* and *Scolosaurus*.

BEGINNINGS—
MATCH BEGINNING CONSONANTS

By this time you should know your dinosaurs. Now find the objects below that match the beginning consonant of each dinosaur shown. See sample under good old *what's-his-name*.

Answers on page 4

T   ___   ___   ___   ___

___   ___   ___   ___   ___

___   ___   ___   ___   ___

T   ___   ___   ___   ___

42

FOOZLE'S FOSSIL FOOTPRINTS!

The fossil footprints Professor Foozle found explain exactly where the dinosaur has gone. Color each footprint with a FOOT in it and you'll know too.

Answer on page 48

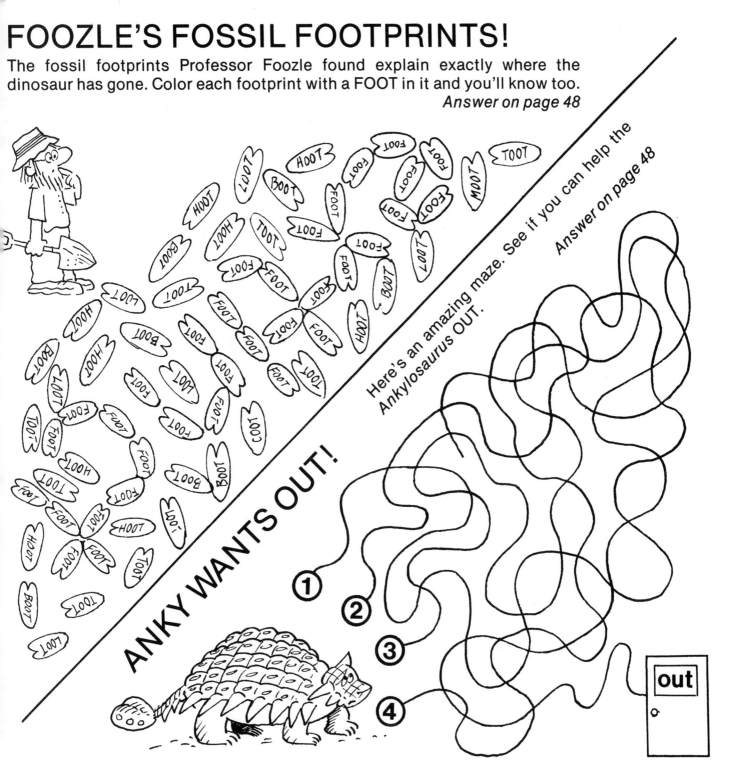

Here's an amazing maze. See if you can help the Ankylosaurus OUT.

Answer on page 48

ANKY WANTS OUT!

out

TRICERATOPS

(try-SER-at-ops)

Triceratops was probably the last of the dinosaurs. This giant, triple-horned beast resembled today's rhinocerous (except in size), but they are not related. The name *Triceratops* means "three horns on the face." It was six to nine meters (20 to 30 feet) in length and just over two meters (about seven feet) tall. Only one of a dozen or more of the ceratopsian or horned dinosaur species, it probably was the largest.

In all ceratopsians the heads are large and the brains relatively small, in a skull nearly two meters (six feet) long the brain weighed only 225 grams (about eight ounces). *Triceratops* lived during the close of the Cretaceous period and near the end of the Mesozoic Age. This was several million years after Brontosaurus and its kind.

An early ancestor was the *Protoceratops* with its great bony frill, yet unarmored except for a thick, tough, scaly skin. The descendants that followed were *Monoclonius* (one horn on the face) and *Styracosaurus* (horn on the nose and a paired series of three horns on each side of the frill). Then *Triceratops,* the largest of them all.

The three horns look menacing but were probably only defensive as *Triceratops* was strictly a plant eater. It had small teeth and a powerful parrot-like beak for chopping and eating tough vegetation.

At the very end of the Age of Dinosaurs, *Triceratops* roamed the plains of North America in herds. We know this from the large number of fossils found.

ANSWERS

FIND THE TRUE TYRANNOSAURUS REX

Page 6

Rex 5 is the true *tyrannosaurus. Rex* 1 is a plant eater. *Rex* 2 has too many fingers. *Rex* 3 is foolish. *Rex* 4 has spinal plates and *Rex* 6 is toothless.

HE EATS LIKE A KING

Page 7

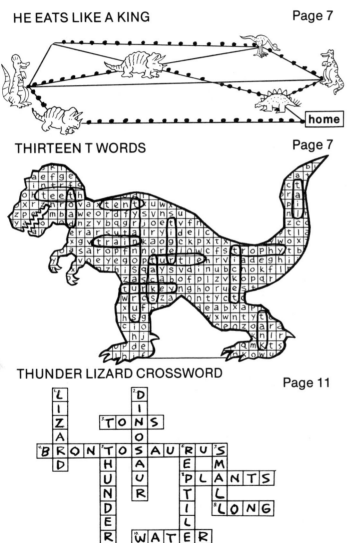

home

THIRTEEN T WORDS

Page 7

THUNDER LIZARD CROSSWORD

Page 11

STEGOSAURUS SCRAMBLE WORD GAMES

Page 1[4]

Game 1

school	apple
guest	ukelele
eagle	raft
goat	umbrella
ostrich	sword

Game 2

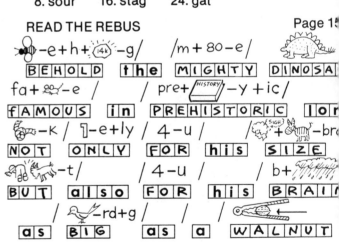

sailor
teacher
beard
greatest
mailbox
artist
aircraft
crutch
tiger
music
horse

Game 3

Page 15

1. oar	9. ruse	17. rag	25. rat
2. soar	10. goes	18. rug	26. sat
3. store	11. rose	19. goes	27. tore
4. guest	12. toes	20. rout	28. tear
5. rest	13. sag	21. route	29. sore
6. rust	14. tag	22. gout	30. stare
7. toga	15. gas	23. got	
8. sour	16. stag	24. gat	

READ THE REBUS

Page 1[5]

-e + h + (14k) -g / /m + 80 - e /
BEHOLD the MIGHTY DINOSA[UR]
fa + -e / / pre + HISTORY -y + ic /
FAMOUS in PREHISTORIC [lore]
-k /]-e + ly / 4 - u / + -br[own]
NOT ONLY FOR his SIZE.
-t / 4 - u / b +
BUT also FOR his BRAI[N]
/ -rd + g / / /
as BIG as a WALNUT

MATCH THE PAIRS

Page 18

Numbers 7 and 13 are pairs
Numbers 2 and 8 are pairs
Numbers 3 and 11 are pairs
Numbers 4 and 6 are pairs

WHICH TYRANNOSAURUS GETS THE MEAL?
Page 19

Spotty gets the meal:

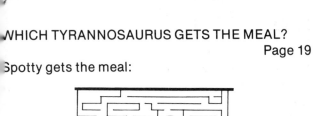

STARRING STRUTHIOMIMUS
Page 25

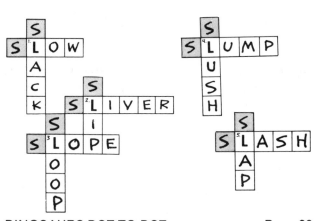

DINOSAURS DOT-TO-DOT
Page 26

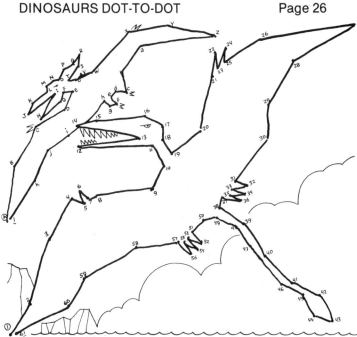

1-10 MYSTERY PICTURE
Page 22

ANTONYMS ANAGRAMS
Page 22

cold	came	walk
cord	cane	wale
card	wane	wade
ward	want	wide
warm	went	ride

MATCH THE ANTONYMS GAME
Page 27

Night/Day, Up/Down, Right/Left, Open/Close
Under/Over, Dumb/Smart, Winter/Summer, Over/Under
Happy/Sad, Smart/Dumb, Down/Up, Day/Night
Summer/Winter, Sad/Happy, Close/Open, Left/Right

NESSIE'S MESSAGE FROM LOCH NESS   Page 30

Message: HAVE NO FEAR, NESSIE IS HERE.
Code answers:
A. Meat eater
B. *Tyrannosaurus*
C. Herbivorous
D. *Brontosaurus*
E. *Corythosaurus*
F. Reptiles
G. Fossil

MATCH HOW THEY MOVE   Page 31

Prehistoric		Present
elasmosaurs	SWIM	fish
amphibians	SLITHER	snake
Pteranodon	FLY/GLIDE	bat
brontosaurs	LUMBER	elephant
tyrannosaurs	LEAP	kangaroo
early reptile	CRAWL	caterpillar
corythosaurs	WADDLE	duck
struthiomims	RUN	ostrich

ARCHAEOPTERYX WORD SEARCH   Page 34

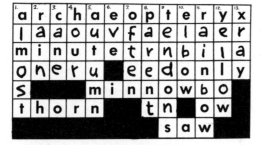

SPEAKING OF FINDING WORDS   Page 34

ADD UP A MESSAGE   Page 35

Some dinosaurs
were no larger
than a chicken.

SEQUENCE THESE PROTO PICTURES   Page

2 - 4 - 1 - 3
4 - 3 - 2 - 1
4 - 2 - 1 - 3
4 - 1 - 3 - 2

PETE PROTOCERATOPS NAMES HIS SON   Page

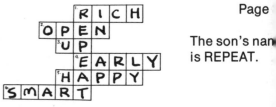

The son's name
is REPEAT.

MRS. PROTOCERATOPS HIDES HER EGGS   Page

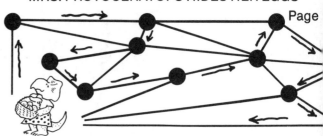

MATCH BEGINNING CONSONANTS   Page 4

FOOZLE'S FOSSIL FOOTPRINTS   Page 4

The footprints spell "extinct."

ANKY WANTS OUT!   Page 4

Trail number 3 leads to "out."

48